# Gabriella's Voice

## The Screenplay

Written by

**Michael J. Vaughn**

EXT; HOUSE; NIGHT

SOUND: A child screaming continuously.

A police car pulls up to the house. POLICEMAN knocks on the door. A middle-aged MOTHER answers.

> POLICEMAN
> Good evening, ma'am. We've had reports of a child being…

> MOTHER
> Abused? Tortured? Murdered? No. That's our screaming child. She's quite good, don't you think?

YOUNG GABRIELLA stands at the window, watching the hubbub. She smiles, proud of herself, then inhales.

SOUND: Soaring soprano aria (sugg. "Ebben? No andro lontana" from Catalani's "La Wally," recorded by Renata Tebaldi)

BILL HARNESS drives an old Pontiac across the Northwestern states — Logan, Utah; the Blue Mountains of Eastern Oregon, the Columbia Gorge at Hood River, and up into Washington State. He leaves a small opera house in Hood River, after a performance, and slips a check into the mailbox. Finally, He crosses Lake Washington on the Floating Bridge and drives over the hill into Seattle. He checks into the Seattle Sheraton.

The next morning, Bill leaves his hotel and walks down the block to the Trademark Café. While standing in line, he spots a flyer for "The Barber of Seville" at the State Ferry Opera Company on Bainbridge Island. He takes the flyer and immediately walks downhill to the ferry depot. He takes a ferry across the Sound, standing on the prow, enjoying the windy trip to Eagle Harbor, Winslow, Bainbridge Island.

INT; THEATER; NIGHT

BILL watches a well-done but decidedly low-budget production of "Barber." He notices that the town "fountain" seems to jump up and down, depending on the theater's sketchy plumbing system. GABRIELLA COMPTON makes her appearance as Rosina, wearing a long brown wig, and Bill is astonished — especially by her cadenza-filled performance of the aria "Una voce poco fa." Afterward, he waits in the lobby with the crowd. When Gabriella finally appears, he shies away, retreating to the back of the room. He writes a large anonymous check, and signs it illegibly. He drops it in a tip jar at the refreshment stand and leaves the theater.

INT; CAFÉ; DAY

BILL enters the Trademark Café, whistling something from the "Barber" overture. GABRIELLA, working behind the counter, turns and smiles. Bill doesn't recognize her.

> GABRIELLA
> Buongiorno, signore. What'll ya have?

> BILL
> Un espresso con panna, per favore.

> GABRIELLA
> Molto bene. Little cioccolata on top?

> BILL
> Mille grazie.

Bill takes his drink to a table and reads a newspaper. An exuberant group of Gabriella's FRIENDS comes in to greet her. Bill keeps looking back. He turns to a review of "Barber," sees her picture, and makes the connection. He arrives at the counter just as her friends are leaving.

> GABRIELLA
> Signore! You've come back.

> BILL
> Si, signorina. I want…

> GABRIELLA
> Muffin? Peanut butter cookie? Refill?

                            BILL
No, I... Are you Rosina?

                         GABRIELLA
                        (taken aback)
Sometimes.

                            BILL
Gabriella, of course.  My name's Bill.  Bill Harness.  I saw
you perform the other night.  You have an incredible voice.

                         GABRIELLA
Grazie.  Look, Bill, I'm sorry if I seem less than delighted, but
I sort of have a Clark Kent complex around here.  I tend to
attract middle-aged men with diva fantasies.

                            BILL
Could I talk to you later?  I'd love to talk to you about your
voice.

                         GABRIELLA
You didn't hear me, did you, Bill?

A CUSTOMER comes in.  Gabriella helps him.  Bill slips a dollar
into the self-serve bucket and gets a refill.  Gabriella finishes with the
customer, then turns to wash some dishes, hoping Bill will go away.
She gives up and turns around.

                         GABRIELLA
Still here, huh?

                            BILL
Yes.

                         GABRIELLA
Need anything else?  Carrot juice?  Almond biscotti?

BILL

Nope.  I'm fine.

GABRIELLA

So.  You want to talk about my voice.  Anything in particular?

BILL

The second cadenza in "Io sono docile" — those bell-like staccatos.  That three-pulse trill you stole from Tebaldi's "L'altra notte."

GABRIELLA

You could have picked that up from a CD cover.  Or one of the regulars at the opera.

BILL

Maybe.

GABRIELLA

Oh.  Hold on.

Gabriella goes to the supply room and returns with a tray of bagels. During the following passage, she puts them into a bagel-chopper and slams down on it repeatedly, particularly when Bill answers a tough question.

GABRIELLA

Name a French opera that takes place in Seville.

BILL

Carmen.

GABRIELLA

Russian opera, same place.

BILL

Betrothal in a Monastery.

                    GABRIELLA
A singer's primary range is known as a…

                    BILL
Tessitura.

                    GABRIELLA
The original name of Rigoletto.

                    BILL
Who is… Triboletto?

                    GABRIELLA
Nice touch.

                    BILL
Thanks.

                    GABRIELLA
Cast me in a major role.

                    BILL
Lucia di Lammermoor.

                    GABRIELLA
Or?

                    BILL
Susanna in "Figaro." Maybe Gilda.

                    GABRIELLA
What about Cio-cio-san?

                    BILL
You're not ready.

                    GABRIELLA
Pronounce Eugene Onegin in Russian.

                    BILL
Yev-GHEN-nee Oh-NYAY-ghin.

                    GABRIELLA
    God.  You're tough.

She picks up the last bagel and points it at him.

    The name... of Tebaldi's... poodle!

Bill reaches into his wallet, pulls out a photo of Renata Tebaldi with her poodle, and places it on the counter.

                    BILL
    New First.

Gabriella means to quietly curse, but it bounces into her singing resonance and echoes around the café.

                    GABRIELLA
    Shit!  Oops.  Don't you hate it when that happens?

                    BILL
    Never happens to me.

                    GABRIELLA
    All right, all right.  You're really into this stuff.  Look.  I've got a meeting with the music director this afternoon on Bainbridge.  There's a coffeehouse called the Pegasus... it's on the waterfront, two blocks from the theater.  Meet me there at six, and we'll talk about my voice.  Just don't turn into a creep, okay?

                    BILL
    Scout's honor.  Addio, Gabriella.

EXT; CAFÉ; DAY

BILL and GABRIELLA sit at a table outside the Pegasus, overlooking Eagle Harbor and its many sailing boats. Gabriella is in full rant, gesticulating as she speaks.

> GABRIELLA
> God! I can't believe it sometimes. I walked into a store the other day and counted 73 CDs of Callas — three of Tebaldi. And you know why? Because Callas was a raving bitch, and Tebaldi was nice. Nice doesn't sell. And affairs with Onassis do. But what the hell does any of this have to do with singing? For God's sake, Billy, say something.

> BILL
> Sorry. I was enjoying the performance.

> GABRIELLA
> Sopranos can be dramatic. So, ask me a question.

> BILL
> What are you doing at the State Ferry Opera Company?

> GABRIELLA
> Why would you ask me that?

> BILL
> Your voice is a rare instrument, Gabriella. Your approach to the acting, the phrasing, is like someone 15 years older. And I swear, I'm a picky listener. I don't go around gushing like this. So what are you doing here?

> GABRIELLA
> Reason one: sheer numbers. Sopranos are a nickel a busload, so you'd better get used to the burn of the branding iron

before you throw yourself into the herd.  Two: politics.  I use some old-fashioned bel canto techniques, and these days, that doesn't always fly.


                              BILL

I wondered about that.


                           GABRIELLA

My teacher is Maestro Giuseppe Umbra.  He is 93 years old, and he worked with Puccini.


                              BILL

You mean he... specializes in Puccini?


                           GABRIELLA

No.  In the early twenties, Puccini was dying of throat cancer.  God!  I have nightmares about that.  It was those damn cigars.  Anyway, Puccini could no longer demonstrate vocal lines for his students, so Maestro did it for him.


                              BILL

So your training comes directly from Puccini.


                           GABRIELLA

I have scores with his notes in the margins.


                              BILL

And the big companies don't like your voice.


                           GABRIELLA

They want belters.  Shouters.  Jumbo-jet nuclear sopranos.  And that's why I'm here.  To study with Maestro, to learn more roles, to get so good they can't ignore me.  So what are you doing here?


                              BILL

Visiting some friends in town.

GABRIELLA

And where are you visiting from?

BILL

Back east.

GABRIELLA

Where? Korea?

BILL

So how about that Ruth Ann Swenson?

GABRIELLA

Jesus, Bill. Here I am pouring out my coloratura heart for you, and you can't tell me one thing about yourself?

BILL

I'm an umpire.

GABRIELLA

Pardon?

BILL

Balls and strikes? Baseball. It's what I do for a living.

GABRIELLA

Oh, yeah. That's believable.

EXT; FERRY; NIGHT

GABRIELLA stands at the rail, enjoying the breeze.

> BILL
>
> You look like the Flying Dutchwoman.

> GABRIELLA
>
> Der Fliegender Hollandfrau! Maestro tells me to ride down below and protect my throat, but how can I when the wind feels like... this?

> BILL
>
> Exactly.

Gabriella realizes something, then jabs a finger at Bill's chest.

> GABRIELLA
>
> You! It was you!

> BILL
>
> What?

> GABRIELLA
>
> That five-thousand-dollar check. That was you!

> BILL
>
> I have no idea what you're talking about.

> GABRIELLA
>
> Oh, Bill Harness, you are a piece of work. Remember The Barber of Seville? I've got some experience with noblemen disguised as poor students. Or umpires. You just better be

the good and sweet Count Almaviva, and not the two-timing, well-dressed Duke of Mantua.

                           BILL
Neither, I swear.  I am but a weak baritone with Tebaldi's poodle in my pocket.

                         GABRIELLA
Yeah, right.

Gabriella drops it, and studies the horizon.

It's so dark out there.  I'd like to gather up all that darkness, swallow it down, piece by piece, and then sing it.

EXT; HOUSE; DAY

OLIVIA stands on porch with a FOUR-YEAR-OLD BILL.

> OLIVIA
> My!  What cold hands you have.

She kneels to put on his gloves, and sings (from Puccini's "La Boheme").

> Che gelida manina!  Se la lasci riscaldar.

SUBTITLE: How cold your little hand is!  Will you let me warm it for you?

Front door opens.  BILL'S FATHER appears, and gives Olivia a scolding look.

EXT; THEATER; DAY

BILL exits the State Ferry Theater after a matinee. It's hailing. He peers out at the weather.

                    GABRIELLA
    So was I good, or not?

Bill thinks he's overhearing someone else's conversation, so he doesn't respond.

    What? Was I that bad?

                    BILL
    Gabriella! I'm sorry. No. If anything, you're getting better. Your breathing has evened out.

                    GABRIELLA
    I'm not deathly afraid anymore. Those cadenzas were scaring the shit out of me.

                    BILL
    I did notice something in the first act, though. You were placing your notes higher in the... what do they call it?

                    GABRIELLA
    The mask?

                    BILL
    Yes.

                    GABRIELLA
    I'm a bit sore today. I had to take it easy till my voice warmed up.

                        BILL

Like a pitcher working through the first innings without his
best stuff.


                     GABRIELLA

Huh?


                        BILL

Sorry.  I'm a bit overfond of baseball metaphors.


                     GABRIELLA

Hey.  After I get out of these goofy clothes, you want to go
somewhere and talk about my voice?


                        BILL

I don't know.  Are you going to turn into a creep?


                     GABRIELLA

I beg your pardon.


                        BILL

Who played shortstop for the Orioles last year?


                     GABRIELLA

Placido Domingo.


                        BILL

Not even close.


                     GABRIELLA

I don't have to be right — I'm a soprano.  The Pegasus?


                        BILL

I've got a better idea.

EXT; RESTAURANT; DAY

BILL and GABRIELLA sit on the back deck of a restaurant overlooking the harbor.

> GABRIELLA
> Damn, Billy!  These are great.

> BILL
> Eating mussels is like ingesting the sea directly.

Gabriella sips her martini and winces (it's her first).

> Drinking martinis is like ingesting gasoline directly.

> GABRIELLA
> Yeah!

> BILL
> It's an acquired taste.  Give it ten years or so.

> GABRIELLA
> So how do you know so much about opera, Billy?  Have you done any singing yourself?

> BILL
> Not professionally.  But I come from a long line of sopranos.

> GABRIELLA
> Ah.  And how come you haven't dropped by the café to see me?

> BILL
> I didn't want to look like a creep.

> GABRIELLA
> Look, son, Gabi's Diva Café is a hard club to get into, but

once you're in, you're in.  So relax.  Did I tell you how
Maestro met Puccini?

                    BILL
No.

                    GABRIELLA
He's nineteen years old.  He's singing "Che gelida manina" at
the festival for Santa Cecilia — the patron sainte of music.
Afterwards, Puccini himself comes up to the stage, with tears
in his eyes, and says, "Where did you learn to sing my music
so beautifully?  You must come and work for me."  Can you
imagine?

                    BILL
I cannot.  But I can tell you how many sopranos it takes to
screw in a light bulb.

                    GABRIELLA
How many?

                    BILL
Three.  One to screw it in, another to say, "I could've done it
better," and a third to kick out the chair.

                    GABRIELLA
Oh God!  You do know sopranos.  Oh!  I'd better get to my
ferry.  Are you coming?

                    BILL
Oh, uh, no.  I'm meeting an old friend from Bremerton.  In
fact, I'm meeting him right here at the restaurant.

                    GABRIELLA
Oh, okay.  Nice seeing you again.  Kiss my hand?

                    BILL
Certainly.

He rises to kiss her hand.  She leaves.  Once she's around the corner,
Bill leaves a bill on the table and heads the other direction, up the hill.

INT; OPERA HOUSE; NIGHT

BILL and GABRIELLA watch a production of "Tosca" featuring a dramatic, wide-mouthed soprano. Gabriella winces at the high notes, pinches his arm repeatedly and, on several occasions, leans over to whisper in his ear. They walk to the lobby, and stop amid a stream of departing opera-goers.

> BILL
> God, Gabi. You are the worst audience-member in the history of opera. Why do you keep pinching me, and what's with "potato"?

> GABRIELLA
> That soprano! She sings with a potato voice.

> BILL
> Potato voice?

> GABRIELLA
> Yeah. She drops her mouth halfway to the turf till it's shaped like a...

> BILL
> I'm guessing... potato?

> GABRIELLA
> Ja. And that enables her to make Neanderthal cave-noises designed to frighten small dogs and get her roles at the Seattle Opera, where Microsoft Millionaires throw roses and laptop computers at her feet.

> BILL
> Okay. But are you capable of simply enjoying an opera?

Can't you turn off the filter once in a while?

GABRIELLA

Follow me.

She leads him into a reception room, to a wall covered in black-and-white photos.

> Oh, look! Licia Albanese — ain't she a doll? Tito Gobbi. Richard Tucker. Anna Moffo. Ah! And Queen Renata. I always feel like I should genuflect. Are you getting the idea, Billy? This is why I'm so picky. This is why I never let up. Because I want to be on this wall. Okay?

EXT; SEATTLE CENTER; NIGHT

BILL and GABRIELLA walk across a wide lawn near the Space Needle.

> GABRIELLA
> You know what I like about you, Billy?

> BILL
> Tell me everything.

> GABRIELLA
> You are the only one besides Maestro who understands what it is I'm doing up there. Do you know how it feels to be working so hard to do something, and have nobody really understand what you're doing?

> BILL
> No.

> GABRIELLA
> When I'm singing just right, I can't hear my own voice. It rings right up out of my head and floats away.

> BILL
> You're missing out.

> GABRIELLA
> I call it my heaven voice. Because you know, when you die, your voice leaves your body and rises to heaven.

> BILL
> Did you get that from Maestro?

                    GABRIELLA

No.  That one's mine.  And it's true.  You want to go
somewhere and get a drink?

Bill eyes the Space Needle.

                    BILL

Let's go up there.

                    GABRIELLA

Oh God no!  Every friend I've got drags me up that silly
thing.  It's just an overpriced elevator ride.  Really.

                    BILL

Rosina, I have a rampant inability to pass up going places I
haven't been.  Come on.  My treat.

                    GABRIELLA

You bet it'll be your treat.


They exit the elevator, into a large room stacked with kitschy
souvenirs.  Gabriella walks to one of the windows.

                    GABRIELLA

That tall, thin building at the end is the Columbia Seafirst
Center, 943 feet tall.  Then my favorite, with the pyramid on
top, that's the Mutual Tower — some groovy Freemason art
deco... "The Magic Flute" as a building.  That little white
spire in the back is the Smith Tower.  Used to be the tallest
building west of the Mississippi.  Then there's the Sheraton,
of course, where you're no longer staying.

She turns to study Bill's reaction.

Why is that, Bill?  Why would you move to Bainbridge and
not mention it to me?

BILL

It just didn't…


GABRIELLA

And you know, someone who knows her role as well as I know Rosina is fully able to spot a familiar face in the audience. So why do you come to every performance and then sneak out during the applause? I'd say you're starting to act like a stalker, except a stalker would have stayed in Seattle, where I spend most of my time. It doesn't make any sense, Bill.


BILL

I'm in love with your voice.


GABRIELLA

Yeah, I know. And I appreciate that, but…


Bill grabs her wrap and pulls her roughly toward him, speaking with a strange intensity.


BILL

I'm in love with your voice, Gabriella. When you perform in that theater, your singing leaves a residue in the air, and I walk the streets of Bainbridge, breathing it in.


Bill notices his hands and loosens his grip. Turning to the windows, he feels dizzy. Gabriella starts crying.


GABRIELLA

I was starting to like you, you know? It's not easy for me to find friends, Billy. I'm weird. I'm obsessed. I'm constructed of different… parts than other people. You might think that's just great, but it's not easy.


Bill stares at the lights of Seattle, which begin to swim as he is overcome by a panic attack. SOUND: a cacophony of soprano music builds in his head, broken by an image: the rear window of an old station wagon being smashed by a wooden baseball bat. Bill takes off, dashing headlong for the elevator. Gabriella watches him, stunned, then runs to the elevator but arrives just after the doors have closed.

GABRIELLA
(arriving on the ground floor)

Bill? Billy!

Bill kneels on the lawn outside, hunched over, his face to the grass, sobbing and gasping for breath. Gabriella runs to him, hesitates, then kneels and pulls his head to her lap. She rocks him and hums "Porgi Amor" from "The Marriage of Figaro."

INT; MOTEL ROOM; DAY

SOUND: Tinny recording of Gabriella singing "Contro un cor," from "Barber."

BILL awakes, finds GABRIELLA at a table, listening to a microcassette recorder. Several tapes are stacked on the table.

> GABRIELLA
> Morning, sunshine. You know, if I find these selling at Tower Records, you're in big trouble.

> BILL
> I... Sorry.

> GABRIELLA
> You know, "Una voce" gets all the attention, but I like this one just as much. Course, my favorite Rossini is "Selva opaca" from "William Tell" — as long as you sing the Italian and not the original French. The French just totally messes with Rossin's rhythms... and...

She gives up her chatter and comes to the bed, dropping her head on the mattress next to Bill.

> Oh, God, Billy. You wore me out. I've never seen someone... snap like that.

> BILL
> It happens... occasionally.

Gabriella gets up, brings him a croissant and a carton of orange juice.

GABRIELLA
Here. From your so-called continental breakfast.

She returns to the table.

You owe me fifty bucks in cab fare and ferry tickets. You also owe me some information. I want us to keep being friends, Billy, but I need a little more to go on. What are you doing here? You gotta give me a few more pieces from this deep dark life of yours.

BILL
Okay. You deserve that. I'll tell you part of it. That'll have to be good enough for now. Let's go somewhere... strange.

INT; CASINO; DAY

BILL and GABRIELLA sit in a dining area near the slot machines, picking over food they've rescued from the buffet.

                    BILL
Interesting spot.

                  GABRIELLA
Something irresistibly cheesy about Indian casinos.

                    BILL
Well, you have provided the setting, now the story's up to me. Let's see. My grandmother had a big ol' laser beam of a soprano voice. She could cut through orchestras like an X-Acto knife through cheesecake. She was raised a Scottish Presbyterian, but one time, she caught the ear of a visiting Catholic bishop. The Bishop was so impressed, he offered her a position singing solos in the big Latin masses at the diocese cathedral. The Presbyterian minister understood that my grandmother's talent was wasted on plodding English hymns — so he encouraged her to take it.

It was a long trip to the cathedral, so my grandmother would spend Saturday nights with the choir director and his large Italian family. For a 17-year-old, it was quite a life. That Easter, my grandmother sang the Messa di Gloria by Puccini — a transposed tenor part, and she was heard by another special visitor — a voice teacher from the Accademia di Santa Cecilia in Rome. The teacher was so thrilled by my grandmother's voice that he offered her a full scholarship and passage to Rome.

For my grandmother, this was a dream come true, for it offered her the chance to study opera. She had spent many of her Saturday nights singing famous arias around her choir director's piano, and she knew that life was leading her toward this new, intoxicating music.

Enter my great-grandmother — willing enough to take money from the Catholics, but not to send her only girl to Rome! "They will make her the Pope's personal soprano!" she complained. "She will sing for him in the morning as he bathes and dresses!" When she discovered scores in her daughter's room with Dago names like Catalani and Bellini – and illustrations of Italian singers in passionate embraces – well, that cut it! Not only could she not go to Rome, but it was back to the Presbyterian Church and "That Old Rugged Cross."

#### GABRIELLA
Yuck!

#### BILL
A few years later, when my grandmother was ready to go out on her own — that was when my great grandmother had her first stroke. It took her seven long years to die. By the time my grandmother was through taking care of her, and then burying her, the operatic impulse was dead, as well. She married a nice druggist, and raised three children. It wasn't till she was fifty, after the last of the kids was off to college, that she returned to voice lessons. She spent the last twenty years of her life appearing in improbably young roles with a patched-together community opera group. Cio-cio-san was her favorite. She died thirty years ago this month.

#### GABRIELLA
But… is that so bad?  She eventually sang, didn't she?

BILL

Ask yourself the same question. Because my grandmother was one of the special ones, Gabriella. She belonged in Covent Garden, La Scala, the Seattle Opera press room — not in church talent shows. Thanks to Great Grandma's stupid bigotries, we'll never know how good she could have been.

GABRIELLA

Fate worse than death.

BILL

I sometimes wish she would have told the old biddy off. But then, I guess I wouldn't be here. Well! That's the family epic — at least, that's where it starts. Give me a while, and perhaps I'll tell you more.

GABRIELLA

Your mother?

BILL

Give me time.

GABRIELLA

Okay.

INT; THEATER; NIGHT

BILL enters the lobby of the State Ferry Opera Company. RODRIGO races in from the auditorium.

> RODRIGO
> Shit! Shit! Shit! Sonafabitch!

He slams the counter, then notices Bill.

> Shit!

Rodrigo storms into the street. Gabriella enters from the auditorium, making ungodly noises.

> GABRIELLA
> Oh! Billy. Sorry. Just taming the monster. I used to scream just like this as a child. I was quite the lil' devil.

> BILL
> I bet. Who's the stormin' Spaniard?

> GABRIELLA
> Oh, Rodrigo? That's Maestro's new tenor. One helluva voice, but lots of control problems. Maestro just got through giving him a good going-over. So. Are you here to spy on us?

> BILL
> Yes. I thought I'd take you up on the offer. You're crazy to do "Figaro," you know.

> GABRIELLA
> Tell me about it! Four hours! And all that ghastly recitative. Well, I'd better get in there. Enjoy!

She kisses him and leaves.

                          BILL
          Be wonderful.

Bill goes to take a drink from the water fountain. JERSEY enters the lobby. They share an odd moment of recognition, even though they've never met. Jersey smiles and enters the auditorium.

Bill watches singing rehearsal (singers standing on stage with scores), fascinated by Jersey. Special focus on her "Voi che sapete."

INT; FERRY DEPOT; NIGHT

BILL and GABRIELLA sit on a bench, waiting for the ferry.

> BILL
> Who's your Cherubino, Gabi?  Was she in "Barber"?

> GABRIELLA
> Of course not.  You came to every performance.  Wouldn't you have noticed?

> BILL
> Yes.  But I still feel like I know her from somewhere.

> GABRIELLA
> Well.  Be careful.  She's got a boyfriend in New York.  Alex is unattached.

> BILL
> Alex?

> GABRIELLA
> Susanna.

> BILL
> But I don't know Alex.

> GABRIELLA
> And you don't know Jersey.  So what's the problem?

> BILL
> But I do know Jersey.

                    GABRIELLA
Oh! There's my boat. Thanks for seeing me off, Billy. And
if you're going to ask out Jersey, keep it discreet, okay?


                      BILL
I… Okay. Good night.

She leaves.

INT; THEATER; NIGHT

BILL watches stage rehearsal. JERSEY enters from the lobby in jeans and her character's bright blue waistcoat. She sits down next to Bill.

> JERSEY
>
> I know this sounds like a line, Bill, but don't I know you from somewhere?

> BILL
>
> No. But I know you from somewhere.

> JERSEY
>
> I thought so.

They watch GABRIELLA singing a scene as the Countess.

> She's got "it," doesn't she?

> BILL
>
> Oh yeah. But so do you — plus a little Red Skelton.

> JERSEY
>
> Harpo Marx?

> BILL
>
> And Carol Burnett.

> JERSEY
>
> Ooh! My heroine.

> BILL
>
> And that first aria — what is it?

JERSEY

"Non so piu cosa, son, cosa faccio." "I no longer know what I am or what I'm doing."

BILL

The second repetition of the last line — "Parlo d'amor con me"? That is so beautiful, the way you back down on that.

JERSEY

God! Do you know how long I've worked on that very thing?

BILL

Hours?

JERSEY

Days. Hmm. Time for me to inject some more hijinks. Pleasure meeting you again, Bill.

They shake hands, but Bill holds on.

BILL

Does Cherubino get any days off?

JERSEY

Tomorrow.

BILL

How'd you like to go on a day trip?

JERSEY

Love to. One catch.

BILL

Si?

JERSEY

Husband.

                    BILL
              (thinks about it)
    I'll be on my best behavior.


                   JERSEY
    Bene. I'll meet you at the Pegasus at nine o'clock.


                    BILL
    Ciao.

She heads to the stage entrance.

INT; CAFÉ; DAY

BILL walks through the rain to the café in Seattle. He enters in high spirits. GABRIELLA is at the counter.

GABRIELLA
Buongiorno. You're flouncing more than a gay tenor.

BILL
I had a wonderful time yesterday.

GABRIELLA
So I heard.

BILL
You did?

GABRIELLA
Si. Oh — hold on a sec.

(to CUSTOMER)

Single latte! Oh, hi. Yes, the cocoa shaker's right behind you. Right there, yes.

(to Bill)

So, yes, I heard you had a good time.

BILL
I was thinking just now that it was the most romantic non-date I…

GABRIELLA
Hold that thought. Georgia?

(to CO-WORKER)

>Could you check the women's room? Someone told me they're out of TP. Thanks.

Gabriella looks back at Bill.

                    BILL
>Um, yes, that it was the...

                 GABRIELLA
              (to Georgia, again)
>Could you check the paper towels, too?

                    BILL
>...best...

                 GABRIELLA
>I'm sorry, Billy. Could we save this for later? It looks like we've got a rush coming. Tell you what. Let me get through this crowd here, then in ten minutes I'll take a break and bring you a cappuccino. Okay? Thanks.

Bill takes a chair, notices that the counter area is not busy at all. A half-hour later, Gabriella arrives with two cappuccinos.

                 GABRIELLA
>Okay, so you had the most romantic non-date, and you had lunch in this cute little historic town on Whidbey Island, and then you hiked the beach at Deception Pass and...

                    BILL
>What are you doing?

                 GABRIELLA
>I'm telling you everything I already know about your date.

                    BILL
     Why?


                    GABRIELLA
     To save you the trouble of telling me.


                    BILL
     Rosina.  How often do I have something new to tell you?
     Don't you think I…


                    GABRIELLA
     Don't call me Rosina in the café.


                    BILL
     Gabriella.  Don't you think I'd enjoy telling…


                    GABRIELLA
     Billy, you know, I'd better get back to the counter.  We're
     short today, and Peaches is kinda new.  I'll be back in a few
     minutes, okay?

She returns to the counter, where there are all of two people waiting.
Bill gets fed up and leaves the café.

As He walks away down the sidewalk, away from the café, Gabriella
steps from the café and yells.


                    GABRIELLA
     You yodeled!

Bill stops and turns.


                    BILL
     Pardon me?

Gabriella charges down the walk, talking the whole time.

GABRIELLA

You went to the ferry shelter, and the next boat wasn't due for an hour, so you started talking with the other people at the shelter, and then Jersey sang "Voi che sapete" for them, and then you got up and... you yodeled!

BILL

And?

GABRIELLA

You told me you didn't sing. But you sing for Jersey? And a bunch of... ferry-waiters?

BILL

I wasn't singing. I was... yodeling.

GABRIELLA
(imitating Jersey)

It was this beautiful old cowboy song, Lonely Yukon Stars. He started out in this lovely floating head-voice, then he did the verses in this sweet, sincere, baritone. Like a Roy Rogers movie. I thought you said he didn't sing, Gabriella?

BILL

I...

GABRIELLA

Why her, Billy? Why not me? She's a mezzo, for Christ's sake! She sings trouser roles. And she never saw you home on the ferry when you had a fucking breakdown!

BILL
(desperate)

All that coloratura has gone to your head!

GABRIELLA

Maybe it has!

                              BILL
        Fine!

                          GABRIELLA
        Fine!

They storm off in opposite directions.

INT; FERRY DEPOT; DAY

GABRIELLA walks up the ramp to find BILL waiting for her. She stops.

> BILL
> Do you have any time?

> GABRIELLA
> Um, yeah. I just have to drop some things off at the theater.

> BILL
> Good. I'd like to tell you a story.

EXT; PARK; DAY

GABRIELLA and BILL walk along a waterfront park (Ft. Ward, Bainbridge Island). Gabriella sees something slithering in the grass.

GABRIELLA

Aigh!

BILL

Don't worry. Just a garter snake. I used to have one when I was a kid.

GABRIELLA

I'm glad you know your reptiles. Are we almost there? I've got rehearsal at six.

BILL

Sorry. Looking for just the right spot. Ah! Here we are.

They enter a clearing next to the water. There's a covered shelter for bird-watchers/fishermen.

GABRIELLA

Ooh! Do you suppose these blackberries are ripe?

BILL

Some. Watch out, though. Even some of the dark ones can be a little…

GABRIELLA

Aigh!

BILL

Tart.

Gabriella gathers a heaping handful of berries and settles on the grass before the shelter. Bill sits on the steps.

> BILL
>
> Let's see, how to start? Give me that red berry.

> GABRIELLA
>
> Really?

> BILL
>
> Yes. It'll help.

Bill bites the berry, makes a sour face, and then begins his story.

> My mother was a soprano. She had the most incredible voice I've ever heard. But she would never sing when my father was around. I could never understand why.

INT; HOUSE; DAY

FATHER heads for the kitchen door, suitcase in hand.

> FATHER
> See you soon, Tiger.  You look after your Mom now.

> BILL, 10
> Sure, Dad.

> FATHER
> Bye, dear.  You've got my number at the hotel?

> OLIVIA
> Baltimore Hilton, Room 227.

> FATHER
> And remember our deal, now.

Olivia makes motion of "zipping her lips."

> Bye now.

> BILL (V.O.)
> But the music was too strong.  Within a week, my mother's voice would begin to break out of its chrysalis.

Olivia hums at the laundry line; sings wordless lines at the sink, does bits of arias in the garden.

> BILL (V.O.)
> By the second week, she was reconstructing entire scenes, singing several different parts at once.  Her favorites were the great death scenes.  Cio-cio-san's hara-kiri.  Mimi's

consumption. The selfless leap of Gilda into Sparafucile's knife. One summer, we had one of those above-ground swimming pools, so she performed Senta swimming off to the Flying Dutchman's ship. Only, it was her notion that Senta would never be caught rising to heaven with a bathing suit on.

Halfway across the pool, Olivia takes off her suit and climbs the steps on the far side, nude. MR. SHORIFF, mowing his back lawn, looks over the fence and nearly has a heart attack.

                          BILL (V.O.)
But her piece de resistance was the mad scene from "Lucia di Lammermoor."

Olivia stands in the kitchen, singing the mad scene, holding a large kitchen knife. She finds a bottle of ketchup and pours it all over her apron. She finishes the scene and collapses to the floor. BILL,10 and BOBBY, 3 erupt in applause.

                          BILL, 10
     Brava! Bravissima!

                          BOBBY, 3
     Lava! Laissi-ma! (or whatever)

Olivia rises from the floor and receives her applause. She takes the dozen roses from a vase by the sink and hands them to the boys. They throw the flowers at her, one by one. She gathers up the roses, bows gratefully, then hands them back to B & B so they can throw them again.

                          BILL (V.O.)
My mother was the greatest of the unknown prima donnas. And the idea of death, in my impressionable ten-year-old mind, became a fascinating and playful thing. I was constantly dreaming up new ways to kill myself. I would be leaning against a brick wall, when suddenly it would collapse, pinning me to the ground as the remaining bricks fell one by

one, beating me into a sheet of pulpy flesh. I would fall through a window, like a hero from an old Western movie, emerging completely unscathed — but then, one small remaining sliver would slip from the windowframe and pierce me in the jugular. This is not unusual. Boys of ten fake their deaths on a daily basis. But they don't sing thrilling, wordless arias as they twist in the wind.

BILL, 10 dangles from a swing, the strap twisted around his neck, singing in a moaning, operatic style, then collapses, lifeless.

My unusual style of play began to concern my teachers, and eventually word got back to my father.

FATHER and OLIVIA sit in counselor's office. Father looks accusingly at Olivia, who shrinks with guilt.

Such discoveries would send my mother into deep depressions. She would lie in her bed for days, and barely speak a word.

OLIVIA lies in bed, her face devoid of expression.

BILL

I couldn't bear living without the sound of my mother's singing. I began to look forward to my father's absences, and to resent his silly rules. After he was gone for a week, I would hurry home from school, knowing that my mother was nearing the bursting point, and would soon be filling the house with glorious sound.

BILL, 10 walks home, enters the house. He finds a sandwich and a glass of milk on the counter, then sits in front of the TV, where BOBBY, 3 is watching cartoons. He looks around for his mom, but doesn't see her. Then he hears the sound of a motor running. He goes out the garage. OLIVIA is in the front seat of the car, dead. BILL, 10 coughs, then opens the big garage door to let in some air. He sits on the steps with his milk, watching.

#### BILL (V.O.)

I kept waiting for my mother to come out of the car, so I could applaud and yell, "Brava! Bravissima!" And perhaps she would sing an encore.

MR. SHORIFF walks by, spots the hose running from the exhaust to the car window. He runs up the drive and pulls on the door handles, but they're locked.

#### MR. SHORIFF

Mrs. Harness? Mrs. Harness! Oh my God. Oh my God!

Mr. Shoriff finds a baseball bat and smashes the rear window. He climbs in, turns off the engine and falls out the passenger's door, gasping for air. BILL, 10 watches, drinking from his milk.

NEIGHBORS gather around. An ambulance drives away.

#### BILL (V.O)

They took me to my grandma's house, and tucked me into bed, even though it was hours before my bedtime.

BILL, 10 gets up from the bed and stands next to the door, listening to the sounds of people below, crying and lamenting.

#### BILL (V.O.)

The people in the house were singing to each other, only it wasn't my mother's kind of singing — it was my kind of singing, the kind I would make up for my death scenes. And I was terribly excited, because I didn't know there were so many people who sang just like me.

It's raining. GABRIELLA sits on the grass, crying. She has ground the blackberries into a pulp, staining her hand. She goes to BILL and buries her face in his shoulder. He lifts a hand to her head.

INT; FERRY DEPOT; NIGHT

BILL and GABRIELLA sit on a bench, waiting for Gabriella's ferry. They both look pensive.

> GABRIELLA
>
> So what was it?

> BILL
>
> She was manic-depressive. Today they call it bipolar. The year she married my father, she had a performance of "Il Trovatore," and afterward, she couldn't stop singing. In the dressing room, at the reception — it was like she was possessed. She started to lose her voice, and they had to give her a sedative. The doctors said that it was the emotional intensity of opera that set it off. A month later, my mother found out she was pregnant. With me. She made a pledge to my father that she would never sing again. But it was too late. The music had already taken hold of her.

They sit on a bench, expressionless. Gabriella goes to a window to look for the ferry, humming something sad from "Figaro." (poss. "Deh vieni, non tardar")

INT; THEATER; NIGHT

GABRIELLA sings The Countess in "The Marriage of Figaro."
(sugg. the garden scene, as she sings to her husband, played by JOE, a
black baritone).

BILL chats with Joe afterward, in the lobby.

> BILL
> So, in your experience, are there more black baritones, or
> tenors, or neither?

> JOE
> Oh, baritones, definitely.

> BILL
> Any particular reason?

> JOE
> We've broken a lot of barriers in casting. But tenors tend to
> be the lovers, the rascals — the sex symbols. And there's still
> a lot of unease about that, especially with all the Caucasian
> sopranos. Like Lily White here.

> GABRIELLA
> What?

> BILL
> We were discussing how beautifully you sang tonight.

> JOE
> Yes. But could you stop knocking me over with that dress?

GABRIELLA

God, I know! It's like navigating a small ship. The HMS Gabriella. Come with me, Billy.


BILL

I follow in your wake.


Bill and Gabriella approach MAESTRO, who relaxes in an armchair.


GABRIELLA

Professore! I want you to meet someone. This is Bill Harness.


MAESTRO

A pleasure to meet you.


BILL

The pleasure is mine. Gabriella talks so much about you, I feel as though we've already met.


MAESTRO

Ah. Gabriella is a good girl.


GABRIELLA
(to Bill)

I have to say hi to someone. Talk to Maestro.


MAESTRO

Gabriella tells me you have been generous to the company. We are very grateful.


BILL

It's the least I could do.


TWO PATRONS come by and congratulate Maestro.


MAESTRO

Thank you. Thank you so much.

BILL

So, Maestro. What is it that makes Gabriella so special?

MAESTRO

You ask a good question. I have always said, to my students: Voice is breath transformed. Now Gabriella, more than any other singer I have known, transforms almost all of her breath into tone. Ninety-nine point nine percent. If my car were so efficient, I would drive to New York on a gallon! Plus, she is determined to work, and learn bel canto. I spoke to Licia Albanese last year. You know her?

BILL

Yes, of course.

MAESTRO

She said, Bless you, Maestro. You are the last of the bel canto teachers. Even in Italy, there are none. And Gabriella, she is my mission, my gift to the world. And she sings beautifully, don't you think?

BILL

Gabriella's voice cannot be described with one word.

MAESTRO

This is a very smart thing you say.

## 22

INT; APARTMENT; NIGHT

BILL and GABRIELLA are tucked into a corner of a rowdy cast party.

GABRIELLA
You know I'm an orphan.

BILL
I...

GABRIELLA
Actually, I can't really say that. I had adoptive parents, but they were older. They died four and five years ago.

BILL
Have you tried to find your birth parents?

GABRIELLA
I'm on a registry, but they can't match you up unless the parents register, too. It's not something I'm waiting around for.

She takes a sip of champagne, looks out at the party.

I picture my father as a practical Irishman, blue-collar — maybe a plumber. But he's got a secret artistic side. Late at night he pulls out a balalaika and plays old Russian folk songs. My mother is sort of a UK mongrel — Scots, Irish, a little Cherokee. She grew up in Little Rock, got bored, moved to St. Louis. Got a job in a blues club in St. Louis, where she met my father. Got pregnant, stayed with some friends in Memphis till she gave birth and put me up for adoption.

When my father returned from the Army, he went back to St. Louis, to that same club, and there was my mom. They live in Duluth, have a son and a daughter in college. My mother crochets and gardens. When she's feeling sad, she sneaks down to the basement and smokes a pipe with raspberry tobacco.

BILL

You've put a lot of thought into this.

GABRIELLA

Had lots of time.

JOE approaches, wearing a mischievous look.

JOE

You know what time it is, Gabi.

GABRIELLA

Oh, no. I'd have to be a lot more drunk than this.

JOE

Dammit, woman! I am the Count. Play for me. You may as well get it over with.

GABRIELLA

Oh, Jesus.

Gabriella fetches a didgeridoo and undoes it from its long cover.

JOE
(to Bill)

Didgeridoo. Australian aboriginal instrument. Ever heard one?

BILL

Never.

JOE

Aye. Then you're in for a treat.

Gabriella plays the instrument like a virtuoso, captivating the party. They follow her into the bathroom, where they "jam," bouncing different vocal tones off the walls.

JOE

You like?

BILL

Fucking incredible!

The party is breaking up. Bill studies the didgeridoo.

BILL

How the hell did you pick this up?

GABRIELLA

Graduation present. I thought, Great — Mom bought me a log. But then I learned what it could do. It's become sort of a tradition at cast parties. Maestro hates it. He calls it "that noisy stick."

BILL

Purist.

GABRIELLA

Speaking of, Maestro wants you to move in with him.

BILL

He… what?

GABRIELLA

He's got a little cottage behind his house.

                    BILL
Well, I couldn't just…

                    GABRIELLA
Don't say no to Maestro.  Once he gets his mind made up…
Besides, you'll be earning your keep.

                    BILL
Doing what?

                    GABRIELLA
Building a deck.

                    BILL
I don't know how to build a deck.

                    GABRIELLA
You will now.

## 23

EXT; YARD; DAY

BILL sits on a half-completed deck, sipping a cup of tea. GABRIELLA approaches.

GABRIELLA
Wow, you did need some work. I can feel the energy shooting out from your face. All pink and healthy.

BILL
I must admit, it feels good. My back is shot to hell, but look! Look what I've made. And it grows by the minute. After this, I'm building a path from here to the back door.

(speaks like Maestro)

"On rainy days, you know, I like to go outside and watch the boats come by. But I am an old man. It is not good to get my feet wet."

GABRIELLA
God! For a minute there, you became an old Italian man.

BILL
Honey, by the time I finish, I'll be an old Italian man. Come spring, we're going to put some boxwood hedges along the far edge.

GABRIELLA
Does that mean you'll be here till spring?

BILL
Yeah. I guess so.

GABRIELLA

Good.

She hugs him.

BILL

So, what do you want for Christmas?

GABRIELLA

A lead role at La Scala.

BILL

So… what do you want for Christmas?

GABRIELLA

Nothing.  Give another thousand to the opera company.

BILL

Two thousand.  Last week.

GABRIELLA

Where do you get all this?

BILL

I'm an umpire.

GABRIELLA

Right.

BILL

I play the stock market.

GABRIELLA

Uh-huh.  Get me a CD.  The "Trovatore" from 1956, Tebaldi
and del Monaco.  Or anything by Patricia Racette.  I've been
meaning to check her out.

BILL

Not nearly enough.  Why don't I take you to the opera?

GABRIELLA

But Seattle doesn't have another production till…

BILL

In San Francisco.

She kisses him.

GABRIELLA

Yes!

BILL

They're doing "Pelleas et Melisande" right after Thanksgiving, with Frederica von Stade.

GABRIELLA

Ooh!  That would be so cool!

BILL

If you're going to be a diva, young lady, you have to stop saying things like that.

## 24

INT; SF OPERA HOUSE; NIGHT

BILL and GABRIELLA walk into crowded lobby at intermission.

> BILL
> God! This opera is so beautiful. The dramatic line is so seamless.

> GABRIELLA
> Through-composed. And it's Debussy's only opera. Isn't that amazing?

> BILL
> Such a waste. Oh, and isn't that Frederica...

> GABRIELLA
> Ooh! I hate her, she's so good.

> BILL
> Scusi, Gabriella. I'm going to queue up for the water fountain.

> GABRIELLA
> I'll be over here, staring at the ceiling.

> BILL
> (looks up)
> I don't blame you.

Bill looks from the line to see Gabriella talking to a short, dark-haired woman. When he returns, the woman is gone.

> BILL
>
> Friend of yours?

> GABRIELLA
>
> Licia Albanese.

> BILL
>
> Oh, right. And I just ran into Arturo Toscanini at the water fountain.

> GABRIELLA
>
> No, really. I took a master class with her last spring. She said I had a classic bel canto voice, that I sang the way she used to.

> BILL
>
> Egad. You don't think of someone like Licia Albanese just walking around like a mere mortal.

> GABRIELLA
>
> She's gotta walk around somewhere. I'll introduce you after the show.

> BILL
>
> I'm so impressed!

> GABRIELLA
>
> Stick with me, baby. You'll meet all the stars.

## 25

EXT; SF OPERA HOUSE; NIGHT

BILL and GABRIELLA exit onto the front steps.

> BILL
>
> I understand the concept, but I've never quite gotten the word.

> GABRIELLA
>
> The Italian is "flowering." It's pretty much the same as "coloratura," except in the lower voices, which can't move around quite so precisely as soprano.

> BILL
>
> Okay. So let me just say, the baritone had a fine fioritura.

> GABRIELLA
>
> Bravo! Oh! What are we doing? We have to find Licia. She was wearing that poofy blue dress.

> STEPHANIE
>
> Kipper! Kipper! William!

> BILL
>
> Stephanie!

STEPHANIE runs up and hugs him.

> STEPHANIE
>
> Oh, Kipper! I thought I'd never see you again. Even your father doesn't know where you are. But you're here! What are you doing in San Francisco?

BILL

Sort of a business trip. I've been doing a… travel research thing for this company in Minnesota. Bed-and-breakfasts, hot-air balloon rides, that sort of thing. What're you doing here?

STEPHANIE

I'm visiting an old college pal. Johnny. Oh, don't get the wrong idea. Johnny's gay. I suppose the whole town is, if you believe my parents.

Stephanie looks toward Gabriella.

BILL

Oh! I'm sorry. Stephanie, this is… Rosina. She's a daughter of an old friend of mine — sort of my unofficial niece. Tomorrow's her birthday, so I promised I would take her to the opera.

GABRIELLA
(takes the cue)
Nice to meet you, Stephanie. Where do you two…?

BILL

Oh! Stephanie. I'm very sorry, but Rosina's father is leaving tonight, and we need to give him a ride to the airport. Can you call me tomorrow? I'm staying at the St. Francis. Just call and ask for my room.

STEPHANIE

Oh. Okay. Damn, it's good to see you, Kipper. I've been worried. But we can talk about this tomorrow. Happy Birthday, Rosina. Nice to meet you.

GABRIELLA

Nice to meet you too.

Bill pulls Gabriella around the corner and hails a cab. They ride in silence.

## 26

INT; HOTEL ROOM; NIGHT

BILL opens the door to their hotel room (not the St. Francis), lets GABRIELLA in, then sneaks behind her, heads for the bathroom, and closes the door. Gabriella hangs up her coat, sits in an armchair and stares at the bathroom door. Eventually, she walks up to it.

                    GABRIELLA
        Billy? Are you all right?

Bill kneels at the toilet, wiping his mouth with a towel.

                    BILL
        Yeah. I'm okay. It was just that Thai food.

                    GABRIELLA
        Vietnamese.

Bill sits in a chair and stares at himself in the mirror.

        Billy? Listen, I'm sure you had your reasons for fibbing like
        that, but don't you think you should tell me? I feel like... an
        accessory.

(silence)

        Billy?

Bill comes out, smoothing his pants legs.

                    GABRIELLA
        So. Are you going to tell me?

BILL

Tell you what?


GABRIELLA

Don't do that, Billy! Don't put me on the opposite side of this... thing.


BILL

What thing?


Gabriella sits on the bed and slaps the mattress, frustrated.


GABRIELLA

Who's Stephanie? Why are you working for a travel agency? Why am I Rosina? Are you going to tell me one goddamn thing?


Bill rubs his forehead, as if he's getting a headache. The soprano cacophony builds, culminating with the image of black-and-white photographs burning in a woodstove. Bill turns and shouts ferociously.


BILL

No! You can't have this one. This one is mine. You've gone too far, goddammit. You can't have any more of me!


He comes to, sees Gabriella on the bed, frightened, and stumbles to the door.


Mi dispiace, Gabriella. I'm sorry. This one... This one will kill me.


He leaves.

INT; BAR; NIGHT

BILL lies head-on-table in the corner booth of a dive bar. BEN, the bartender, approaches.

> BEN
>
> Buddy! Hey.

> BILL
> (waking)
>
> Huh?

> BEN
>
> Closin' time. You want me to call you a cab?

> BILL
>
> No. Right up… street. Jesus! I feel… sober.

> BEN
>
> Y'had two Manhattans and fell asleep.

Bill pulls himsclf to his feet

> BILL
>
> God. I can't even get drunk properly.

He hands Ben some money.

> Grazie, Beniamino. Buona notte.

> BEN
>
> Yeah, thanks.

Bill walks uphill, nearly gets run over by a bus, enters the hotel.

INT; HOTEL ROOM; NIGHT

BILL slips into the room. GABRIELLA is watching television. She turns it off.

GABRIELLA
You want to yell at me some more?

BILL
No. I'm sorry. It's the music, you see. I am a victim of Music Poisoning Syndrome. You think music is a benevolent force, and it is… but you see, anything taken in excess can be toxic. And I am a child of the soprano voice. It's killed off the rest of my family, and now it's finally come for me. Vicious thing, the opera.

GABRIELLA
You're drunk.

BILL
No. Oh, I tried. Because I know, no matter what I might have… yelled at you before, it's time to tell you the rest of the fucked-up Harness family saga, and believe me, honey, it's a stinkeroo.

He sits on the bed and puts a hand on Gabriella's face. He notices she's been crying.

I'm so sorry.

GABRIELLA
Oh, Billy! I worried about you. I don't know what I'd do if you weren't around.

BILL

I'm not the type for suicide, Gabi. Much too... operatic.

GABRIELLA
(laughs through tears)
Good. So, if you told the story, would it take some of the poison out of your system?

BILL

I don't know; I'll have to try... But I can't tell it if I can see you. And you need to be absolutely silent. This is so ugly, the only way I can tell it is if I can convince myself that nobody else is in the room. Here, let's try this.

Gabriella sits on the chair inside the bathroom. Bill pulls the armchair to the bedroom side of the same wall, and leaves the bathroom door open. He sits down, and tries to gather his thoughts.

GABRIELLA

I have to go run some errands, Billy. I'll be back in an hour or two.

She turns off bathroom light.

BILL

Buon viaggio, Gabriella. That brilliant light that was my mother — none of it got to me. My light was left in shards on the floor of our garage. I became a bland, overanxious boy. The light passed over me and landed on my little brother, Bobby, who was too young to process ideas like mental disease and suicide.

Bobby was a born leader. People gravitated to him. He had a wonderful sense of humor, a way of putting people at ease. He would have been a great politician. But he lacked ambition. For years, he would get jobs through sheer force of personality, then quit them six months later when he got bored.

His only real ambition was to be happy, and there was one place he was always happy — the ballfield. He'd played baseball all his life, and followed the Red Sox with a passion. So he became an umpire. He was a great umpire. In ten years, my brother never once ejected someone from a game. He could sense when a player was about to blow his top, and could defuse him with the slightest joke, or smile. The message was, "Isn't this an absurd little game? But isn't it a fun little game? Could you think of one other place you'd rather be?" Bobby was magic.

He especially loved working with kids — because that's where it all started, that's where you could instill this idea of fun before the screaming parents and overzealous coaches screwed it all up.

In romantic matters, Bobby was about as uncatchable as a good knuckleball. Some girl would come around with one of those oversized catcher's gloves, would have him right there in her sights, and then whipp! Bobby would catch a draft and duck right past her, all the way to the backstop. But then came Stephanie.

## 29

EXT; BALLFIELD; DAY

Slowpitch softball game. STEPHANIE waggles her hips in the batter's box, drawing attention from BOBBY and the CATCHER. The first pitch comes inside, and she has to step back.

>                    STEPHANIE
> Blue! Did you see that? This guy's throwin' at my head!

>                    CATCHER
> Crowdin' the plate. Had to brush you back.

>                    BOBBY
> Just don't go rushing the mound. The pitcher would only enjoy that.

>                    STEPHANIE
> I'll bet.

Next pitch bounces off the top of the catcher's glove. He turns around and runs off to fetch it.

> See that big gap in right-center, Blue? I think someone needs to plug it.

She rockets the next pitch to right-center, all the way to the fence, and slides in with a triple. She dusts herself off and shoots a "finger-pistol" toward Bobby.

Later. Long fly to left. Stephanie snaps it into her glove.

>                    BOBBY
> That's game!

PLAYERS line up to shake hands. Bobby goes to the backstop to write the score on a clipboard.

                    STEPHANIE
        Yo, Blue!

She tosses the ball to Bobby.

                    BOBBY
        Thanks!

                    STEPHANIE
        Good game.

She trots off. Bobby watches, then looks at the ball, which reads "Stephanie," followed by her phone number.

                    BILL
        Bobby was in love. He and Stephanie spent the next five
        years circling each other like twin suns, and we all looked
        forward to the day of their wedding. A day that would never
        come. Every time Stephanie brought up the idea, Bobby put
        up another wall. We had misread something about Bobby,
        and Stephanie was paying the price.

EXT; HOUSE; NIGHT

STEPHANIE shows up at BILL's door, crying, hysterical. He takes her inside.

### STEPHANIE
I gave Bobby an ultimatum. He…

She breaks down, crying on his shoulder.

The next morning. Bill wakes up in bed, next to Stephanie.

### BILL
I might have done it because Bobby had stolen my mother's light. I might have done it to make up for my own failures. But mostly, if sleeping with me gave Stephanie some measure of revenge, then so be it. In the morning, I gave her a brotherly kiss on the cheek and sent her on her way. I didn't see her again until the funeral.

EXT; BALLFIELD; NIGHT

SAMMY FARGO stands at the plate, BOBBY umping behind him.

> BILL (V.O.)
> Sammy Fargo was having a bad day. The man was a dead-on slugger, but today he had two neurons firing incorrectly, and that was enough to throw off the whole operation.

Sammy takes a monstrous swing and hits a weak grounder to the pitcher. He stops five feet out of the batter's box, bat still in hand, as PITCHER fields the ball, notices Sammy stopping, then rolls the ball to first base for the out.

> BOBBY
> The batter is out, and the pitcher is a real asshole!

EVERYBODY laughs — except Sammy, who walks back to the dugout, smoldering.

Later. SAMMY and MANAGER confer at the on-deck circle.

> MANAGER
> Sammy. Tying run on second. All we need's a single. So relax. Nice, easy swing.

Sammy lunges at the first pitch and hits a weak fly behind third base. He trots toward first, eyeing the ball. BOBBY follows the ball, too. LEFT FIELDER catches it. Sammy swings the bat with one hand, in frustration, but loses his grip. The bat flies toward home plate. Bobby lies on the ground near home, dead.

EXT; CEMETERY; DAY

> BILL (V.O.)
> Two hundred people gathered to watch the Harness family lower its final shaft of sunlight into the ground. Sammy Fargo was not among them.

CROWD disperses. BILL and STEPHANIE find each other and embrace.

INT; HOUSE; DAY

FATHER piles dishes into a box.  BILL enters from the garage.

> BILL
> Hey, Dad.  I'm going to start on the rec room, okay?

> FATHER
> Yeah, go ahead.  I'll be down here a while.


BILL enters the rec room and sets a box next to the trophy case, filled with photos and appreciation awards.  He starts wrapping them and setting them into the box, but stops when he hears an odd noise from one.  He shakes the trophy next to his ear, then finds a bolt underneath and loosens it, prying open the hollow part of the trophy to discover a wad of hundred-dollar bills.  He undoes another trophy, and finds another stash.  FATHER enters to find Bill on the floor, surrounded by disassembled trophies and a huge pile of cash.  They sit at the kitchen table, around a bowlful of money, drinking coffee, doing nothing, saying nothing.

> BILL (V.O.)
> We were afraid to do anything.  We were afraid of what we would find next.  No umpire in the world makes that kind of money.


BILL climbs to the rafters of the garage, finding a pile of neatly stacked umpire-shirt boxes.

And no umpire in the world needed fifty brand-new shirts.

He opens a box, takes out a shirt, and finds a plastic bag filled with black-and-white photos. He pulls them out.

Children. With each other. With faceless adults. Doing everything you could imagine.

FATHER and BILL sit at the kitchen table, drinking coffee around the bowlful of money. Unopened shirt-boxes line the counter. Father sets down his mug.

FATHER
Here's what we're going to do.

BILL sits next to the woodstove, taking the photos out of the boxes, tossing them into the fire.

BILL (V.O)
I spent ten hours at that woodstove, burning it all, a day-long column of grilled obscenities. It was mid-summer; burning photochemicals don't smell good at all. It's a miracle nobody stopped by to check on us. But the Harnesses, they'd had a death in the family, you could forgive them a few... eccentricities.

BILL picks up a final box, this one made of wood. He looks inside to find pictures of Bobby with children. He opens the woodstove door, too soon. Flames fly out as he shoves the whole box inside.

He stands in the bathroom, toweling off after a shower, then looks in the mirror to discover that he has singed off his eyebrows. His hands are marked by blisters and bruises.

Following V.O. accompanied by images of Bill's travels, his attendance at a small opera company, and him driving in a rainstorm in Tennessee.  At final line, returns to him in the hotel room, silhouetted in darkness.

BILL (V.O.)

Dad was a tax accountant — a damn crafty one.  He put the cash into an untraceable account.  I taught myself an illegible signature.  For two years, I have been crossing the country in Bobby's old Pontiac, seeking out promising young singers and donating to their companies.  We wanted to take that money and reverse its polarity, maybe even use it to plant some of my mother's sparks in the music halls of America.

It occurred to me, somewhere in the middle of Tennessee, that, during that night with Stephanie, I was punishing my brother for his one civilized act.  Somewhere under that well-crafted veneer, he understood what kind of monster he was, and knew that he was unfit to marry and bring children into the world.  So he told Stephanie no.  And we never told her a thing.  Her dream lover remains intact.  As for me, I will never feel completely clean again.

## 34

INT; COTTAGE; DAY

It's raining.  BILL sits at his table, aimless.  A knock.  He goes to the door.  It's MAESTRO.

> BILL
>
> Maestro!  Buone sera.  Come in, please.

> MAESTRO
>
> Bene, bene.

He sits in a rocking chair before the fire.

> You will excuse me, please.  I am very distracted.  My new tenor, Rodrigo.  His throat has been kissed by God, but he throws it away.  He is a note-hunter.  He creeps up from below.  He thinks he is Sinatra singing "Witchcraft," and all the pretty girls will swoon.  He also taps his foot when he sings — so he is Astaire, too.  But when people hear his voice, they will forget.  That is what I tell myself.  And you, my friend, how are you?

> BILL
>
> I am not so well, Maestro.

> MAESTRO
>
> You miss Gabriella?

> BILL
>
> Yes.

> MAESTRO
>
> Gabriella is your angel.

### BILL

Angel, muse, siren. I can't narrow it down to a single mythological being. I am a man made of Swiss cheese, and it's not that Gabriella fills those holes — but she makes them smaller. She gives me something to believe in.

Maestro takes a poker and stokes the fire.

### MAESTRO

I know for a fact that Gabriella is your angel. She wanted to cancel this "Fledermaus" to stay here with you. She says you have opened an old wound for her sake, and now it will not heal. It is much money, this Fledermaus, and a good contact. That is how much she cares for you. Me, I don't care for you quite so much. I tell Gabriella no, you cannot go back on your word. You go to Vancouver. I will keep an eye on your friend.

### BILL

Thank you, Maestro.

### MAESTRO

Gabriella tells me you saw Albanese in San Francisco?

### BILL

Yes.

### MAESTRO

Do you know how Albanese made her debut?

### BILL

No.

### MAESTRO

She is 17, she has trained all her life — she knows already five major roles. She is in Parma, on tour, watching the older singers perform "Butterfly." Before the third act, Licia's teacher comes and tells her, "The soprano has fallen sick. You must sing Butterfly." So she does, and she sings beautifully, and eventually she sang that role more times in New York than any other singer, ever. Because she is small, has dark hair — she is the perfect Cio-cio-san. Now. Let me see your palate.

### BILL

Pardon?

### MAESTRO

Like with the dentist. Open and say "Ah." Oh, see, this I know. You have a tenor's palate — high and even. And you have a singer's soul — they are all a little Swiss cheese, you see. You come take lessons with me. I bring you a voice.

### BILL

Perhaps I will. But Maestro, this story about Albanese. No offense, but was there a point to it?

### MAESTRO

Some stories have a point, some... entertainment. That one — entertainment. Now. I have a job for you, because you need one. I want you to make this for me — on the deck, for my singers.

Maestro places a chart on the table. Bill studies it.

### BILL

Grazie, Maestro. I'll start right away.


A few days later. It's sunny. BILL has finished his work and, as reward to himself, rides a bicycle through Winslow to the Pegasus Coffeehouse.

## 35

INT; COFFEEHOUSE; DAY

BILL enters and finds GABRIELLA behind the counter.

BILL

Gabi?

GABRIELLA

Billy!  Buongiorno.

Bill takes Gabriella's hand and covers it with kisses.

Billy!  I'm trying to make a latte.

BILL

I can't tell you how good it is to see you.

GABRIELLA

Yes you can.

BILL

It's really goddamned good to see you.

A SQUAD OF CYCLISTS walks through the door.

GABRIELLA

Damn!  A rush.  Let me get rid of these guys, and we'll talk.
There's so much to tell you.

BILL sits at a table.  GABRIELLA arrives with two cappuccinos.

Oh, Guglielmo.  I've been so worried about you.  On New
Year's Eve, I pictured you in the audience, with that small,

steady smile, drinking in each note.  So.  Here's the latest. Maestro is taking me on full-time — especially now that we're doing "Tosca."

(talks like Maestro)

"Tosca will be your breakthrough.  Tosca will make you a prima donna."

Oh!  So I'm moving into his guest room.  We're going to be neighbors, Billy!

                    BILL
Great!  That'll save you a lot of ferry-time.  But what are you doing here... at the Pegasus?

                    GABRIELLA
The owner's a big opera fan.  When she heard I was a barista, she made me a standing offer.  And now, I'm taking it.  So what have you been up to?

                    BILL
Would you like to see?  When do you get off?

                    GABRIELLA
Seven.  And I've got a lesson at eight, so I was headed to Maestro's, anyway.

                    BILL
Great!  I'll meet you out front.

## 36

EXT; HOUSE; NIGHT

BILL meets GABRIELLA, takes her to the backyard. He throws a switch, and the deck lights up — a labyrinth outlined in roped lights.

> GABRIELLA
> Oh my God! It's gorgeous. What is it?

> BILL
> It's a labyrinth. For meditation. Go ahead, give it a try. You enter it right here.

Gabriella walks the loops, mesmerized.

> GABRIELLA
> You really have to pay attention.

> BILL
> That's the idea. It gives you a simple, immediate task, and takes everything else out of your mind. This one's based on a turf labyrinth in England called The Walls of Troy. In Scandinavia, they use this type of labyrinth to capture the spirits of the dead. You see, the spirits travel only in straight lines, so if you get them to enter the labyrinth, there's no way for them to get back out.

Gabriella achieves the center, stomps her foot and sings "Non la sospiri" from Act I of "Tosca." Bill listens as the aria morphs into the soprano cacophony of his panic attacks. He starts breathing hard, then runs to the end of the deck. Gabriella follows, finds him at a spot overlooking the water. He lies with his face to the planking, crying. A full moon cuts a path of white across the Puget Sound. Gabriella kneels and brings her head to his lap, kissing his hair.

GABRIELLA

That wasn't so bad as the other ones.

BILL

No. Do you know, Gabriella, that you have my mother's voice?

GABRIELLA

I thought maybe.

BILL

You do. I didn't realize it before.

GABRIELLA

I take that as the highest of compliments.

Pause. He studies the moontrail.

BILL

When I was young – eight, I think – my mother and I were sitting next to a lake in upstate New York. She told me that the moontrail was actually made of milk — magic healing milk, produced by a rare species of underwater jersey cow. And these aquacows would only produce their special milk at night, and only when the moon was out. And "why was that?" I asked. And she said, "Why, Billy, because they have a strong union."

As you can imagine, to milk these cows directly would take some doing, what with the cost of scuba gear, pipelines, and water-resistant alfalfa. So the locals would wait till the milk rose to the surface, then ride by in boats and scoop it into their tanks.

"So how come this milk isn't available at the supermarket?" I asked. My mother replied that the dairy farmers were very protective of their simple way of life, and feared that if they sold the milk to outsiders, big mega-milk corporations would come and build ugly offshore milk platforms. Even so, she said that she had once ventured out into the moontrail herself to scoop up some of the magic healing milk, and that she kept it in a secret place inside our house. She said she only brought it out when I or my brother was sick.

GABRIELLA

Did it work?

BILL

The way my father tells it, my mother would heat up some milk and then drop in a touch of vanilla extract and a splash of blue food dye. It had a remarkably positive effect on our recovery times.

GABRIELLA

I love your mother.

BILL

Do you know, in Celtic tradition, the center of the labyrinth is thought to be the meeting place of heaven and earth?

GABRIELLA

That's what it felt like. That's why I started singing. Is it okay if I sing again?

BILL

Yes.

Gabriella sings a couple phrases from Ponchielli's "La Gioconda."

What is that?

GABRIELLA

"La luna discesa nel mar." The moon descends into the sea.

Later. BILL is walking out of the labyrinth, speaking to GABRIELLA as he keeps his eyes on his feet.

                    BILL
        When do you move in?

                    GABRIELLA
        This weekend. Will you help me?

                    BILL
        Of course. Then I will take you to dinner, to the swankiest, most expensive restaurant in Seattle.

                    GABRIELLA
        Where's that?

                    BILL
        You tell me.

                    GABRIELLA
        Pagliacci's.

                    BILL
        No!

                    GABRIELLA
        Yes.

                    BILL
        That's too perfect.

He reaches the end of the labyrinth. Raises his hands.

        I'm out!

## 37

EXT; COTTAGE; NIGHT

GABRIELLA arrives at BILL's door dressed as a Parisian artist, circa 1860.

> BILL
> Bon soir! I'm guessing Rodolfo?

> GABRIELLA
> Always wanted to be a tenor. Here. I brought these for you.

She hands him a top hat, a long coat and a scarf.

> BILL
> I'm either Colline, or Abraham Lincoln.

> GABRIELLA
> Colline. And don't go singing to your coat.

They arrive at Pagliacci's in a horse-drawn carriage.


INT; RESTAURANT; NIGHT

BILL and GABRIELLA have polished off a great meal.

> GABRIELLA
> Oh God! I don't know what we're going to do with Rodrigo. He is absolutely the worst actor to ever set foot on an opera stage.

> BILL
> As long as he opens his mouth and sings…

GABRIELLA

That's what everybody keeps saying.  So.  I have to tell you now.

BILL

Tell me what?

GABRIELLA

About Licia.  She's coming, Billy!  To opening night.

BILL

Really!  That's wonderful.

GABRIELLA

That's not all of it.  If she likes what she sees, she might present me next autumn at her New York recital.

BILL

That does it.  Waiter!

WAITER answers Bill's call.

WAITER

Yes, sir?

BILL

Two things.  First, this bill is nowhere near high enough. Second, we must celebrate this young woman's ascendancy into the firmament.  Now you tell me:  What does that add up to?

WAITER

Forty-year-old tawny port from Lisbon.  $60 a glass.

BILL

Magnificent!  We'll take two.

GABRIELLA

Billy?  What is this all about?

BILL

As soon as I pay this bill, Gabi?  It's gone.  It's all gone.

GABRIELLA

Congratulations.

EXT; FERRY; NIGHT

BILL and GABRIELLA stand at the railing.

> GABRIELLA
>
> What are you going to live on?

> BILL
>
> I'll be okay.

> GABRIELLA
>
> What did you do for a living?

> BILL
>
> Umpire.

> GABRIELLA
>
> I thought that was a joke.

> BILL
>
> It was — I wasn't very good. But before that, I was in finance. I made a lot of money. I'll be fine.

EXT; RESTAURANT; NIGHT

BILL sits alone at an outdoor table, finishing a martini, looking out over the waterfront of Bainbridge Island. He takes a last swig and begins his walk uphill to the theater.

EXT; THEATER; NIGHT

BILL spots the silhouette of MAESTRO, chatting with LICIA ALBANESE. Bill approaches them.

MAESTRO
Ah! Here he is now. This is William Harness. Bill, this is Licia Albanese.

BILL
Signora Albanese. I can't tell you how many hours of pleasure you have given to me and my family.

LICIA
Grazie, grazie.

She sizes him up.

You are right, Professore. I can see it in the eyes, the lips.

MAESTRO
Licia thinks she once performed with your mother.

LICIA
Oh! I am sure of it. It was 1951. Or 52. I was doing a guest appearance with an opera company in Albany. Your mother was performing Susanna, but during my visit she stepped aside so I could play the role instead, and she played Barbarina. Well! She sang that little aria, "L'ho perduta." Like a human bird she sang, so tender, so effortless, the way she handled her line, her dynamics. And the light poured from her face, like nothing else mattered so much as this one little song. I turned to the director and said, "My time is

wasted on this one." "Why?" he said. "Because," I responded. "I cannot teach her a thing." Whatever happened to her?

BILL
She had… medical problems, and had to leave the opera.  She died a few years later.

LICIA
I am so sorry.  Aigh, what a waste!

The theater lights flash.

MAESTRO
We had better get inside.

BILL
Thank you, Licia.  I can't tell you…

LICIA
You're more than welcome, my dear.

INT; THEATER; NIGHT

The first two acts go beautifully, especially RODRIGO, who is suddenly acting like Deniro.  In the final torture scenes between himself and Scarpia (played by JOE), Rodrigo is sweating, pale — genuinely suffering.

EXT; THEATER; NIGHT

BILL walks outside at intermission and finds flashing lights. An ambulance is driving away. MAESTRO paces up and down the walk.

> MAESTRO
>
> William! I am so glad you are here. It's Rodrigo. During the torture scene, when he was offstage, he became suddenly ill. He threw up. It is a miracle he could go back and continue. I have rarely seen something so heroic. After the scene, he collapsed. The paramedics, they think it is food poisoning. They say he will be all right. But he is gone, and I fear we must cancel the last act. We are a small company, we cannot afford understudies, Bill. Oh, this is very bad.

> BILL
>
> No, Maestro! Not tonight.

> MAESTRO
>
> But what can we do? There is no third act without Cavaradossi, without "E lucevan." We cannot send Gabriella out to sing with air!

> BILL
>
> Where is she? Does she know?

> MAESTRO
>
> How could she not? She's in her dressing room.

BILL passes through the backstage area, past a costumed FIRING SQUAD, up the stairs to GABRIELLA's dressing room. She lies atop a pile of wardrobe, crying. Bill kneels next to her. She turns her face to his jacket.

GABRIELLA
Oh, God, Billy. Have you seen Rodrigo? Is he all right?

BILL
He's very sick. But I think he'll be okay. Do you think Licia heard enough?

GABRIELLA
No. It has to be perfect. I wouldn't blame her at all, either. She has to have her standards, and this is very... unprofessional, let's face it. It's not going to happen this time. I'll just have to wait a little longer.

Bill hands Gabriella a Kleenex from her makeup table, then wanders the stacks of wardrobe, thinking.

BILL
What if I sing the third act?

GABRIELLA
Billy, if that's your idea of a joke...

Bill sings the climactic line of "E lucevan" ("Oh! Dolci baci, o languide carezze...") in a soaring tenor voice. Gabriella shoots to her feet.

Billy? Is that... you?

Bill sings the Act I response to Tosca's entrance: "Son qui." ("I am here.")

MAESTRO whisper-shouts from the bottom of the stairs.

MAESTRO
Rodrigo? Did I hear Rodrigo?

Gabriella leans through the doorway and whisper-shouts back.

GABRIELLA
Maestro! Billy's going to sing Cavaradossi.

MAESTRO
And I am Ricky Ricardo!

GABRIELLA
Let him explain later. Go out and tell the audience we have a substitute tenor for Act Three. Go! Presto!

Maestro leaves, muttering in Italian.

What's your waist, Billy?

BILL
Forty.

GABRIELLA
Forty. Painter. 19th century. Marcello! Joe's a little beefier than you, but here's a belt. If that doesn't work, you'll have to sing with one hand on your pants. Forget the makeup, we don't have time. Meet me at curtain left and...

(hugs him)

Oh, Billy. You had one more story, didn't you?

BILL
It killed my mother, Gabi. I just couldn't do it anymore.

She lets go and points a finger at his nose

GABRIELLA
Five minutes. Curtain left. Be sure you've got a ring to bribe the guard.

BILL

Si.

Bill puts on his costume and peers down through a mirrored window at the audience settling down, and the orchestra preparing, as Maestro can be heard explaining the company's predicament. Bill walks down to the backstage area, company members watching him as he goes. SOUND: the music begins. Bill reaches curtain left, where Gabriella waves him toward the GUARD.

BILL<br>(to Guard, in a hushed voice)

Will you be my escort?

Guard nods, takes him by the arm. STAGE DIRECTOR gives them a cue. Guard pushes him roughly out to the stage (in character). They fade into the stage lights as the audience applauds in appreciation of the emergency fill-in.

# Critical Praise for
# GABRIELLA'S VOICE,
## The Novel:

"Michael J. Vaughn has turned out a beautiful, lyrical novel. I was caught up in the narrative within three sentences and was held spellbound by the story until the end. It is as captivating as a well-performed *La Boheme*, as tragic and triumphant as *Tosca*."

— Ani Harrison, *Tacoma Reporter*

"By turns rousing, lyrical and intoxicating, GABRIELLA'S VOICE is the work of a virtuoso."

— Calder Lowe, *The Montserrat Review*

"Vaughn performs the… task of invoking sounds from the silence of words on paper. Arias whirl from the pages… a treat for the ear as well as the mind."

— Gregory Harris, *BookPage*

*Available everywhere fine books are sold.*